GROOVY GRAN
and the
Karaoke Kid

Written by Janine Scott
Illustrated by John Bennett

In memory of my grandad,
Bill (William) Mackie

For Rosie, Molly, Gracie, and Eadi,
who make life unpredictable in a groovy way!

CONTENTS

CHAPTER 1

Gran and Her *Horror*scopes!

Monday, May 28
Dazzling – that's you now, with your stars
more brilliant than a thousand comets.
You're in the spotlight for fame and success.

My grandmother – Gran for short – likes to read the horoscopes every morning during breakfast. But not even the best horoscopes could have predicted what was going to happen to me over the next week. If I'd known that I would be driven to school by someone who thinks she's a Formula One race car driver, go shopping with a bowlegged cowboy, and sing karaoke at the mall, I probably wouldn't have bothered to get out of bed.

Gran is Mom's mom. She's slightly nuts. Well, that's what Dad says anyway. Mom says she's not nuts; she just has a creative streak.

"Hear that, Billy? Fame and success!" said Gran that morning.

I could tell Ruby, my younger sister, was about to say something smart, but she was stopped by some juice from her grapefruit. It hit her in the eye. Gran kept on reading despite Ruby's shrieks.

Gran's horoscope said her day would be full of surprises. That's nothing new. She always tells me that a surprise a day keeps boredom away.

"Hurry up, Geena. It's eight o'clock already," yelled Mom from downstairs.

My big sister is not a morning person.

Dad came down, with tissue on his shaving cuts. "Does anyone want a ride to school?" he said.

I jumped up and kissed Gran good-bye, leaving her to her horoscopes.

"Enjoy your day of fame and success," she said.

"I will, Gran," I called from the back door.

I didn't want to disappoint her, but I knew that Ms. Hathaway's class was not going to bring me fame and success. It never has before.

And I was right. Ms. Hathaway started off the morning by handing out our poetry test from

Friday. I had done badly. By the look of everyone else, the rest of the class had done badly too. Everyone, that is, except Megan Butler.

Then Ms. Hathaway made us pair up to select and prepare a poem to read aloud to another class. Gran's prediction of fame and success was about to be proven wrong for the second time. Ms. Hathaway paired me with Seth Ryan, who thinks he's too cool to read poetry, and far too cool to read it with me.

After lunch, we piled into Mr. Washington's classroom to present our poems. Seth and I were the last to read. When I started, everyone laughed. Seth had chosen a T. S. Eliot poem about a cat named Mungojerrie. It wasn't until I caught a glimpse of Seth out of the corner of my eye that I realized exactly what was happening. Seth was mimicking me behind my back. Unfortunately, Ms. Hathaway couldn't see what was going on, and before Seth could read his part, the bell rang. Seth was off the hook. But, luckily, not for long.

Later, before Ms. Hathaway dismissed class, she announced her next idea – a talent contest to be held next week. At least Seth wouldn't be able to escape that. Then again, neither would I.

After school, I go to Mom's work. She's a nurse at a retirement home nearby, and she pays me an allowance for helping out. So, while Ruby's afternoons are filled with dance class and gymnastics, mine are filled with pouring cups of coffee for the residents as they play cards or listening to the veterans' war stories. All the residents love me. They pat my head and say what a great boy I am. Mom gets a kick out of it.

"Oh, Grace, what a fine-looking boy you have," Mildred tells Mom every single day. Of course, Mildred can't see past the end of her nose.

The retirement home isn't all bad. Sammy Starbright is fun. He's a male version of Gran. He loves the limelight. But I'm not sure if Gran and Sammy would like each other if they met. Ms. Hathaway says that opposites attract, so I suppose Gran and Sammy would repel. They'll never meet anyway. Gran doesn't like retirement homes and says that she hopes she is run over by a bus, or struck by lightning, before she has to go near one.

When I arrived at Mom's work after school, my head was spinning because of the talent contest. Ms. Hathaway had really done it this time.

"Hey, kid," yelled Sammy from a chair on the porch. "Why the long face?"

"Dumb old school," I replied.

"What about it?" asked Sammy.

"First it's poetry reading. Then it's a talent contest. Where does Ms. Hathaway get these ideas?" I moaned.

Mom was giving Hector his medication and spotted me. She came over to see what I was complaining about.

"Billy, I hope you're not tiring out Sammy," she said in her nurse's voice.

"No, not at all, Grace," said Sammy.

I was glad that he didn't tell Mom about the talent contest, because I wanted to keep it from her and Dad. I didn't want them to come.

"So, kid, here's your chance to be rich and famous," said Sammy.

"I doubt it," I said. "I'm thinking of singing a song, but I'm not very good."

Before Sammy could say anything more, Mom came over, rattling her car keys.

"It's time to go, Billy. I need to get some groceries. You'll see Sammy tomorrow," she said.

Sammy gave me an it-will-be-OK wink as I slouched out the gate toward Mom's car.

Over dinner, Gran told us how her horoscope had come true. She had been surprised to see an old friend riding past on a bus when she came out of the gym. All through dinner, she talked about Samuel Fogerty, the old friend on the number seventeen bus. Luckily for us, Gran's stories were funnier than most of the ones I was always hearing at the retirement home. Dad even chuckled, which was the second surprise, as he tries not to encourage her odd ways.

The third surprise was when Gran found out that my day hadn't brought me fame and success.

CHAPTER 2

An Albatross around My Neck

Tuesday, May 29
I don't really need to tell you that you're
one of the most attractive signs in the zodiac,
but now you're about to show it! Admirers
flock to be close to you.

Gran was up with the sun and even more chipper than usual. She wanted to see if she could track down Samuel Fogerty. When I came down to breakfast, she was busy calling the downtown bus terminal to find out the route of the number seventeen bus from Branston. While she was waiting for the person to check the timetable and streets, she chatted about the day's horoscopes.

"Billy dear, watch out for admirers crossing your path."

"OK, Gran, I'll watch out," I said, not believing her again.

"Hey, Gran, what's going to cross your path?" Ruby piped up as she tried to get a segment of grapefruit without squirting herself in the eye.

"I hope it's Samuel Fogerty, not the number seventeen bus," said Gran, laughing.

"What?" asked Ruby.

"It's a joke, goofball," said Geena, not even bothering to look up from her magazine.

Ruby didn't talk for the rest of breakfast.

"Hey ho, here I go!" said Gran, putting down the phone. "Gran's Surveillance and Detective Agency is open for business."

She went upstairs to get ready and came down five minutes later in something eye-catching. Unlike most detectives, who wish to remain inconspicuous, Gran wanted to be noticed, at least by Samuel Fogerty. And, in her flowery shirt and leggings covered with stars and moons, he'd notice. Unless he's as myopic as Mildred is.

"I spy with my private eye," Gran sang as she waltzed out to the garage, swinging her handbag like a lasso, "something beginning with *S*..."

"Silly, scatterbrained, skittish..." I muttered.

"Bye, Billy dear, my gorgeous grandson!" she shouted.

"Bye, Gran. I hope you find the something beginning with *S*," I yelled back.

"Bye, Geena. Bye, Ruby. My darlings!" She had to yell above the noise of her VW Beetle, which is another reason why Gran would be noticed. The car has red and black spots and is covered with hand-painted ladybugs. Gran, Ruby, and I did the paint job last summer when we were bored one afternoon. Gran made me print the name *The Flying Beetle* on the car because she thought her writing was too spidery.

I daydreamed about last summer while Mom drove us to school. If Mom's car had a name, it'd be *Myrtle the Turtle*. She's a slow driver. But this morning, I was in no hurry to get to school early. I'd just have to listen to Megan Butler talk about the talent contest if I did.

By the time Mom finally pulled up outside school, I had about two minutes to spare. I got to my seat just before I heard Ms. Hathaway's shoes clip-clop into the room.

"All right, class, this morning is devoted to practicing for the talent contest," she said, giving Seth her Hathaway-look as he arrived at class late. "I'll come around shortly to write down what act you've decided to perform."

Talk about a variety show. Who would have thought that in Ms. Hathaway's class lay hidden a magician, an impersonator, and even a juggler. But Seth's idea was the most extraordinary. I heard him say that he wanted to perform a song from the musical *Cats*. I knew then that Seth was up to something. He was more the long-haired rock-star type than the long-haired Mungojerrie type. I was going to find out exactly what he was up to. But it would have to wait because Ms. Hathaway was making a beeline for me.

At lunchtime, my friends Mitch and Josh were off practicing their mime act. I sat outside eating my lunch, waiting for the admirers to flock to me as Gran had predicted. But only Megan Butler, pecking at her sandwich, walked past. As I ate my surprise sandwiches – Gran's way of keeping the boredom out of school lunches – I noticed that

Ellie Ferrari had a flock of admirers hanging around her, and I knew why. Not only was Ellie pretty and smart, she was a lot of fun as well. The problem was, whenever I went to talk to her, I got nervous and said something stupid. Unfortunately, Seth had an adoring flock encircling him too. Ellie and Seth were the most popular kids in school.

The flocks took flight when the bell rang. Afternoon class was uneventful. Well, almost. I spotted Seth talking to Christopher Preston, a boy from the next grade. It struck me as strange because Christopher was not the type Seth would be seen with normally. They were in the library with their heads together, whispering. Seth was definitely up to something, and I was going to find out exactly what it was. But it was going to have to wait until tomorrow. Seth was, once again, saved by the bell. We were all dismissed for the day.

On the way to the retirement home, I wondered whether Seth and Ellie would pair up for life like swans do. But my thoughts were soon interrupted by the dazzling sight of Sammy Starbright, banjo in hand. There he was at the front gate, decked out in flared trousers, a ruffled shirt, a sequined bowler hat, and a banjo.

"Howdy, kid. Ready to start your singing lessons?" he asked in a singsong voice.

"Ummm… well…" I hesitated. "It's not quite what I had in mind, Sammy. I was after a more upbeat street look."

"Ah, well. We'll worry about the special effects later. I'll strum, you hum," he said, playing a few chords on his banjo.

It was all going too fast for me. Up until yesterday, the only singing I'd done was along with the radio in *The Flying Beetle*, Gran's stereo on wheels.

"Couldn't you go first?" I pleaded.

"OK, kid. I might be a little rusty though. I haven't sung in public since the war."

But as Gran says, rust never sleeps, and she should know. *The Flying Beetle* has one or two spots under the ladybugs. Once he got started, the rusty Sammy turned into a well-oiled singer. Soon a flock of cardplayers and tale-tellers were on the lawn, clapping their hands and tapping their feet.

Mom came to see what was going on.

"What's this? Opera in the park?" she joked.

"I was just showing Billy…" said Sammy.

"Showing me how he can still hit the high notes," I interrupted.

"Well, I hate to break up your fun, but you and I need to make tracks, Billy," she said.

"Phew," I muttered under my breath.

"Meet me at the car, Billy. I need to talk with Patti. I have a suggestion to put to her," said Mom, making her way to the manager's office.

"Well, kid, Sammy Starbright's School of Singing is now officially open," sang Sammy.

Maybe Gran and Sammy were made for each other after all.

During dinner, Ruby was acting like Megan Butler – a real pain. I had to put up with her trying to drop hints to Mom and Dad about the contest. She'd heard about it from one of her friends.

"Learned any good songs lately, Billy?" she said, snickering, as she shoveled peas into her mouth.

Before I could answer, Dad scolded, "Don't talk with your mouth full, please, Ruby."

This was the perfect diversion. Gran leaped in telling us about who had crossed her path that day. And, by the sound of it, just about everyone had. Her morning started off with chasing the number seventeen bus along its route leading to Branston. Then *The Flying Beetle* broke down on the other side of town, and she had to take the number fourteen bus to get part of the way back. On the bus, she sat next to a girl who licked an all-day lollipop. Then, when Gran got off the bus, she was followed by an overfriendly dog that had picked up the scent of the girl's lollipop. I think the dog must have drawn her off course because she got a little lost, and, finally, she was brought home in a police car. Gran was really pleased about that because it gave her a chance to get some tips on how she should track down Samuel Fogerty.

Dad wasn't so pleased. He had to vouch for Gran, then sign a piece of paper the way you do when a package from a delivery company gets brought to your door. If Gran had been a package, Dad would probably have sent her back with "Return to Sender" stamped on her forehead.

Dad went on to tell us that the police thought that Gran might be showing signs of dementia, partly because of the way she was dressed, partly because she didn't know exactly where she was when they picked her up, and partly because of the way she was acting, which, by then, was a little odd. But I suppose they would have thought that.

They weren't used to Gran and her ways. Dad soon straightened them out.

After dinner, while I loaded the dishwasher, I imagined what it would be like having flocks of people around you the way Seth, Ellie, Gran, and Sammy almost always did. Despite what my horoscope predicted, I imagined myself as an albatross, flockless, destined to lead a lonely life. So after I had put everything away and kissed Gran good night, I slunk off to bed early, feeling that loneliness and the talent contest were like an albatross around my neck – a real burden.

CHAPTER 3

Uh-Oh! A Duo

Wednesday, May 30
Your public image is on the verge of a beautiful transformation. If you want to get somewhere in life or achieve an ambition, then looking good is vital to your success.

After a restless night's sleep, I went down to breakfast bleary-eyed.

Unfortunately, Gran had recharged her batteries overnight and was livelier than ever.

"Billy sweetheart, wear your red sweatshirt today. You look good in it," she suggested. "Your horoscope says that your public image is on the verge of a beautiful transformation."

She made it sound as if I were about to turn into a butterfly.

"OK, Gran. Just for you," I said, knowing that Ellie wouldn't notice me, no matter what I wore.

I walked to school alone. I needed to figure out how I could win Ellie over, as well as figure out what Seth was up to. Near the entrance, I saw Seth waiting. I hoped it wasn't for Ellie.

"Hello, Seth," I greeted him as I passed.

"Hi, Billy-boy," he replied, sneering.

Then I heard him say hello to someone behind me. A male voice answered.

"Is everything OK?" whispered Seth.

"Yeah. It's all set," replied the mystery person.

"Great," said Seth.

If I wasn't mistaken, the mystery person was Christopher Preston, but I couldn't be certain because when I glanced back, Seth was surrounded by his adoring flock. On the way to class, I tried to figure out what "It's all set" could mean. But I soon had other things to think about, such as how to make it through a morning of rehearsals.

It was like the buildup to opening night on Broadway – chaos. Megan Butler was rushing around trying to organize the props for everyone, and Ms. Hathaway was running around trying to calm everyone down. I wanted to escape and head home, but I still had afternoon classes and singing with Sammy to get through.

At lunchtime, all that Mitch and Josh could talk about was the talent contest.

"How's your act going, Billy?" asked Josh.

"It's not," I said. "I just can't get into it at all."

"Why don't you give us a sneak preview?" said Mitch. "Josh and I might be able to help."

"Thanks, but someone is helping me already," I told them, leaving it at that. I wasn't about to tell them that the someone was an old man who dressed in ruffles and sang cabaret songs.

As I walked to the retirement home, I tried to think of excuses I could use to put off practicing with Sammy. Before I could think of anything, the words "Hey, kid!" brought me around.

"Hi, Sammy. What brings you out to the gate?"

"I'm eager to get started, that's all," he said.

First, though, Sammy told me about a concert Patti was organizing for the retirement home. Mom had come up with the idea when she saw Sammy singing on the lawn. Sammy agreed to be the star attraction, but only if he sang in a duo.

"Great," I said when I heard the news. "So who is the other singer?"

"Here's looking at you, kid," he said.

"ME? ME!" I yelped. "No way!"

"Look, it'll be a good dress rehearsal for you," he said. "It'll help build your confidence for the big night."

"Well," I groaned, "I hope you're right."

By the time Mom came to get me, Sammy's banjo had had a good workout. Sammy was a great teacher, even if I wasn't such a wonderful singer. He said that I just needed to relax. But how could I, with the talent contest looming?

When Mom and I got home, Dad and Ruby were making dinner, Geena was in her room, and Gran was out. As soon as Ruby saw me, her eyes lit up. She was almost bursting at the seams.

"I know something you don't know about Seth!" she taunted when Mom had left the room. "Marisa and I discovered it today."

Marisa was Ruby's best friend and, of all people, Seth's sister.

"So?" I replied, sounding uninterested.

"So, wouldn't you like to know what I know?"

"I couldn't care less about Seth and what he's up to!" I fibbed.

All through dinner, Ruby talked about Marisa. In the end, Dad silenced her by telling her to do less talking and more eating.

After dinner, while Gran and I played basketball in the driveway, I found out that her investigation work wasn't going much better than my singing. Samuel Fogerty, last sighted on the number seventeen bus, had disappeared without a trace. However, Gran didn't seem down about it. In fact, later on, when I went to bed, she was still following up other lines of inquiry. She was on the phone to her best friend, Marjorie Harrison. If *anyone* knew *anything* about *anyone* in *any* part of this city, it was Marjorie!

CHAPTER 4

Groovy Gran and Hip Lips!

Thursday, May 31
Get ready to shake, rattle, and roll on your
most romantic day so far this year. You are
the source of hidden talents and sparkling
conversation. How can you fail?

Gran could hardly contain herself when I sat down to breakfast. Marjorie had given her a few good leads, and Gran was eager to follow them up.

"So, Gran, do you think you'll meet your sweetheart today?" I asked.

"No, that's what *your* horoscope says, darling," said Gran. "Mine says that I'm going to travel."

"Well, just make sure you don't travel in a police car this time," joked Mom as she ate her grapefruit.

"Grace sweetheart, I might be home late tonight, but I'll be with Marj, so don't worry about me," said Gran as she went to grab her car keys from the hall table.

"Good luck, Gran," I called out to her.

"Good luck to you too," she said, giggling and blowing me a kiss from the hallway.

"Wait a minute," Mom called after Gran, "I forgot to ask. Can you drop off Billy at school? I've got to take Ruby and Geena to the dentist before work."

"Sure. He can keep Marj and me entertained with his sparkling conversation and hidden talents," agreed Gran, laughing.

"Hurry up, Geena. We'll be late," yelled Mom from the bottom of the hallway stairs.

"OK! OK!" snapped Geena, who was in the bathroom trying to make herself beautiful.

"You hurry up too, Ruby. I'm leaving in five minutes, and don't forget to brush your teeth."

I only had time to give my teeth a quick brush. Gran was in a hurry to pick up Marjorie so that they could begin their surveillance work. Marjorie lives nearby in a replica of a fourteenth-century castle. Her late husband was a stonemason and crazy about medieval architecture. He was the type Mom would describe as having a strong creative streak. Marjorie, who's far from medieval herself, acts like a teenager. When Gran and I picked her up, she was wearing lime green cargo pants and an orange-striped T-shirt, with a pea-patterned scarf flung around her neck. Gran and Marjorie really are like peas in a pod when it comes to the way they dress.

"Hop in, Marj!" shouted Gran as she came to a halt outside Marjorie's. "Samuel Fogerty awaits."

Gran roared off with Marjorie and me sharing the backseat. The front seat was taken up with the surveillance equipment: a pair of binoculars, a thermos, and a wicker picnic basket – the contents of which were tied down. Gran takes corners far too fast, making her sandwiches a real surprise.

Luckily for me, the trip didn't last long. By the time I'd asked Marjorie about her week, Gran was at the school. She came to a stop right next to, of all people, Seth and Ellie. I climbed from the backseat, past the surveillance gear, and out through the passenger door, trying to make sure that I didn't knock Gran unconscious with my arms and legs and schoolbag. When I finally made it to the sidewalk – on all fours – Gran blew me kisses and Marjorie had her lips smacked up against the car window. Then they left as they had come. Well, not quite. The window on Marjorie's side was plastered with orange lipstick marks.

"Groovy gran you've got there, Billy-boy. She could drive Formula One cars at Indianapolis," said Seth, laughing.

"Uhhh… yeah…" I mumbled. "Real groovy."

"And that was a cool grandma in the backseat. Very hip lips!" joked Ellie.

"Hmmm… yeah…" I stumbled on. "Real hip."

Then I was horrified to hear the sound of a familiar car reversing toward us. I glanced around to see *The Flying Beetle* again. Marjorie was soon performing the same maneuver I had pioneered moments before. Unlike me, she managed to end up standing on two legs. She stood there, waving my school lunch, which I had purposely left on the backseat. I'd had enough surprises without having to eat Gran's sandwiches as well.

More kisses and fond farewells from Gran and Marjorie followed, then silence at last – well, apart from the giggles of Seth and Ellie, who were walking off hand in hand toward class. I slouched ten paces behind, knowing that I hadn't impressed them with my sparkling conversation as my horoscope had said I would. But it could be said that I had a hidden talent for getting out of a tiny car driven by my Formula One grandmother and codriven by a one-in-a-million Marjorie.

During the morning, we all practiced our acts. It was pretty chaotic, and Ms. Hathaway was looking tense. Megan Butler, who has *never* hidden any of her talents before, tried to keep her act under wraps. She found it nearly impossible.

During lunch, Ruby and Marisa followed me around the playground, snickering and whispering something about Seth's closet.

"He has a big cat in his closet," Ruby said finally. She couldn't contain herself any longer.

"So what!" I snapped back, thinking that he could have a lion in his closet for all I cared.

Having two giggling girls follow me around was totally uncool, especially when the girl I was trying to impress was watching. Luckily, I managed to give Ruby and Marisa the slip when their teacher stopped to talk to them. I wish I could have given Sammy the slip that afternoon. At least then I wouldn't have ended up making a fool of myself in front of Ellie for the third time in one day.

As I was walking up the wheelchair ramp leading to the retirement home, Sammy came out onto the porch to greet me.

"Hi there, kid! Ready for some fun?" he asked.

"Sure thing, Sammy," I answered, hoping that his idea of fun would be the same as mine. I soon found out that it wasn't.

"I thought that we should immerse ourselves in music," said Sammy. "Why don't we go to the music store at the mall? I've already asked Grace, and she says it's OK with her. So how about it?"

"All right, Sammy," I agreed, thinking it would get me out of singing practice.

On the way, Sammy insisted on a detour to the secondhand clothes store. He thought it would be a good place to create an image for my act. Why he thought that, I'll never know. When we walked inside, I was almost knocked out by the smell. It was a mixture of moldy old shoes, stinky shirts, and mothballs. It reminded me of some of the closets at the retirement home. The citrus air freshener that the store manager was spraying around when we walked in made it worse. I began to think that Sammy and I might have different ideas about the kind of image I wanted to create.

"Come here, kid," he called, motioning me over to a shirt rack. "What do you think of this?"

He was holding up a flowery shirt with a collar that was so wide you could have made it into a tie or something. It was horrible.

"Let's keep looking," I suggested politely.

Eventually I had to get some fresh air, so I left Sammy rummaging through the racks. He came out looking like a rodeo rider, wearing fringed suede pants, a vest, and cowboy boots.

When Sammy and I walked into the music store several minutes later, I thought that Sammy was finally on my wavelength. This was definitely *the* place to create a rock-star image. Even the guy stocking the shelves looked as if he should be on stage smashing guitars. Mind you, I'm sure Ms. Hathaway wouldn't approve of me snarling out a song and wearing yellow-tinted sunglasses, my hair orange, and my ears pierced. But I guess the music store manager was a lot different from Ms. Hathaway.

Up until then, I had been too busy worrying about creating my image to worry about the effect that Sammy and I were creating right now. When I looked around, I noticed that everyone was staring at us. I suppose it was because Sammy was still trying to break in his boots. He walked kind of bowlegged, as if he had just ridden into town on a horse. When the shelf-stocker saw us, he pointed in the direction of the country-and-western music section in the back. That's probably why I didn't notice Seth and Ellie come into the store. But it wasn't long before they noticed Sammy and me.

When Sammy saw the cabaret CDs, he started acting like a kid in a candy store. Then he turned into what Dad says Ruby can be like – a bull in a china shop. He started bumping into things. I think it was because he was still trying to get used to the heels on his new boots. The display stand with the jazz CDs toppled over first, which started off a domino effect, ending with the stand right next to Seth and Ellie.

"Stand back, everyone!" yelled Sammy to all the customers.

I turned around just in time to see all six stands go crashing to the ground. Sammy and I dived to the floor and started picking up the CDs. That's when I recognized Ellie and Seth's shoes among those of the crowd.

"Hey, kid, when I give you the word, do what I do," Sammy whispered to me.

"OK," I answered, feeling happy that his long life had trained him to think fast under pressure.

"NOW!" said Sammy in a loud whisper.

I crawled on my hands and knees, following Sammy out through the maze of legs. Then we got up and made a dash for the door.

I galloped back to the retirement home while Sammy returned at a slow trot. His boots were beginning to hurt him. Luckily, Mom didn't seem to notice that we were both a little shaken up. In the end, I pushed Sammy – who by then had blisters as big as silver dollars on each heel – in a wheelchair up the retirement-home ramp.

Later that night, even Gran's tales about her surveillance work that afternoon seemed tame compared to my experience of shopping with Sammy. When I went to bed, the flashbacks from my day with Marjorie and Gran and Sammy seemed like a bad dream. The memory of hearing Seth and Ellie laughing, however, was my worst nightmare.

CHAPTER 5

One Sammy and Five Rubys

Friday, June 1
Romance is in the air. You'll have a close
encounter with someone whom you have
admired from afar. If you want to create
a fresh, bright image, then now is the time.

"Today you're lucky in love, Billy dear," said Gran as she skimmed over my horoscope.

"Oh, really?" I said, *definitely* not believing her this time, especially because part of today's horoscope had happened yesterday. Dad's right when he says that horoscopes are like weather forecasts – they're usually a day off.

"Yes, I can feel it in my bones," said Gran.

Knowing my luck, the close encounter would be with someone ancient, like Ms. Hathaway.

All through breakfast, I thought about the talent contest instead of yesterday's disaster at the music store. In the time it took Ruby to eat her grapefruit, Gran to read the horoscopes, Mom to drag Geena out of bed, and Dad to cut himself shaving, I realized that Sammy was right about my needing to immerse myself in music before the talent contest. I was just going to go about it differently.

After dumping out my cereal when Mom wasn't looking, I went upstairs to get my portable CD player, then I crept into Geena's room while she was in the bathroom. I flipped through her CDs, picked out a new one, and left everything almost as I had found it.

On the way to school, it was fun sitting behind Geena in the backseat of Dad's car and listening to her CD. She didn't suspect a thing, not even when I had to crank up the volume because I couldn't hear the music over Ruby's singing. It was lucky for me though. Geena has nails as long as daggers, and she wouldn't hesitate to use them on me if she found out that I'd been snooping around in her room and borrowing her things.

When Dad dropped Ruby and me off at our school, I spotted Seth and Christopher Preston talking near the bike racks. I'd been so busy with Gran, Marjorie, and Sammy – trouble really does come in threes – that I'd forgotten I had wanted to find out what those two were planning. Unfortunately, Seth also spotted me.

"Hey, Billy-boy. That's one cool grandpa you have. A perfect match for your groovy granny," called Seth. "He even dresses the same."

My last little shred of hope that Seth and Ellie might not have recognized me at the music store yesterday faded.

"No… he's not…" I started to explain. Before I could set him straight about Sammy not being my grandfather, Seth walked away laughing, with Christopher following behind like a puppy.

So off I went, vowing I'd wipe the smile off Seth's face once I'd figured out what he was up to.

I still hadn't come up with any answers by the time I got to the retirement home that afternoon.

"Hey, kid," called Sammy as I walked up, "you're early. Eager to get started?"

"Yeah, I suppose I am," I said, referring to being early, not eager.

"Great! That's what I like, an enthusiastic student," he said, bubbling over with excitement.

During my lesson, I found myself actually beginning to enjoy singing with Sammy. But the fun soon came to an end.

"What's that?" I asked, looking at what Sammy was proudly holding up as I took a gulp of my juice during a break. Singing was thirsty work.

"Your costume for our duet," he replied. "You haven't forgotten it's in two days' time, have you?"

"I can't wear that!" I shrieked.

"Why not? I did when I was your age."

"The pants are too short, and the hat is totally silly!" I said, hoping the horoscope didn't mean this when it mentioned a "fresh, bright image."

"Of course! If you want to sing like a star, you have to dress like one," he explained. "And, if I'm going to be a star, you have to be one as well. We're a duo, remember?"

"All right, all right," I agreed, "but I'll be wearing something less bizarre for the contest."

"That's fine by me, kid," he said, looking pleased with himself. "Now, see if it fits."

So there I was, standing in the very same costume that Sammy had worn as a boy, just as Mom came into the room to tell me that it was almost time to pick up Ruby from her dance class. Mom's eyes sparkled as brightly as Sammy's costume. She laughed so much that she almost drowned in her own tears. It was so embarrassing. How could I talk my way out of this one? Luckily, I didn't have to. Sammy did it for me.

"So what do you think, Grace? I dug it out for old times' sake," he explained to Mom.

While I was standing there, self-consciously trying to hide behind the jeans and T-shirt I was clutching in my hands, Mildred came in to ask Mom something. Despite her failing eyesight, Mildred never, ever misses a thing. She's the retirement home's busybody. Keep in mind, you could hardly miss me.

"Billy, you look splendid," she cried out. "Hey, Ethel, come and see Billy. Don't you just love him to bits? Isn't he a looker?"

Unfortunately, Mildred not only has poor eyesight, she also has bad hearing, so she shouts.

Mildred's shouting and Ethel's running attracted Charlotte. It was the first bit of excitement in the retirement home in ages. Mildred and her friends had come to check me out in Sammy's costume.

"If only I were seventy years younger," Ethel shouted to Charlotte, whose hearing was only slightly better than Mildred's. "He's quite a catch."

"Who needs to be young?" Charlotte joked.

Mom could hardly contain herself.

"I wish my late husband had looked like that when he was Billy's age. Someone's going to fall in love with you, young man. You just wait and see," yelled Mildred.

"Someone already has," said Mom, laughing.

"Really, dear? Who's the lucky girl?"

"Me!" snorted Mom, thinking she was funny.

I looked over at Sammy for some male support, but he just shrugged his shoulders and gave me a don't-fight-it-if-you're-outnumbered look. Mom finally rescued me from what was turning out to be another humiliating experience.

"Come on, lover boy. We have to get to Ruby's class, but I think you'd better change first."

I slipped into the bathroom to change my clothes, and, even in my old jeans, I walked out to a chorus of "See you later, gorgeous!" and loud hoots of laughter.

In the car on the way to Ruby's dance class, I tried to convince Mom to keep quiet about the costume, especially to Ruby. It would have been the cue that Ruby needed to spill the beans about the talent contest. Mom and Dad were still in the dark about it, and that's how I wanted it to stay.

"Please, Mom," I said. "Not a word to anyone!"

"OK, lover boy. Mum's the word!" she said.

As we pulled up outside the dance studio, Mom asked if I wanted to come in. Normally, I'm happy to wait in the car. Watching Ruby isn't exactly my idea of fun. But then I remembered my music immersion plan. Unfortunately, this was part of it.

"OK. It would be good to check out how Ruby's coming along," I told Mom, which sounded pretty unconvincing. Mom knows that I'm never interested in what Ruby does, and vice versa.

"Are you feeling all right, Billy?" she asked.

"Never better," I fibbed. I was beginning to feel the strain of the last few days.

Mom and I crept in quietly and stood at the back of the class. We watched eleven girls and two boys dance around the studio. There seemed to be lots more than that because the walls were covered with mirrors. I could see five Rubys waving at Mom, which was scary. One was too much for me most of the time.

I began to regret my music immersion plan. The noise was deafening. Ms. Munro, the dance teacher, was even more deafening. She looked like a delicate ballerina, but she had the personality of a school bully and the voice of an army drill sergeant. Yet I suppose anyone who can keep Ruby under control gets my respect.

"All right, everyone, that's it for today. Now, remember, if you're late for class next time, you'll have extra exercises. No excuses, do you understand?" she lectured.

"Y-e-s, M-s. M-u-n-r-o," the class chimed.

"OK then. Dismissed!" she shouted, storming off like a commando.

Ruby came rushing over to us. She wanted to show Mom the stuff she'd learned in class. While Ruby danced in front of the mirrors for Mom, I hung around, regretting stepping out of the car.

I had always thought that modern dance meant exactly that, but what I saw was far from funky. It was a cross between ballet and tap dancing, and definitely not what I had in mind for the talent contest. In fact, it was about as far away from a fresh, bright image as you could get. While I waited, I leaned against one of the mirrors, with my legs crossed at the ankles and my thumbs hooked into the belt loops of my jeans, trying not to look as awkward as I felt.

"Hi there," said a girl with red hair who was Ruby's age. "Ruby didn't tell me about you."

I'm sure Ruby didn't even tell her that she had a brother. She's always telling me that she wishes I didn't exist.

"Oh, you know Ruby," I said. "Her mind's always on other things."

"Well, if I had a brother as good-looking as you, I'm sure I wouldn't forget," she said, smiling.

I could feel myself turning as red as her hair. If Sammy had been here, he'd have given me one of his looks. Thankfully, I wasn't alone for long. Ruby and Mom wanted to get going. Phew!

We drove away from the dance studio a couple of minutes later and passed the redhead, who was walking home and tossing her hair from side to side like a supermodel. When she saw me – even though I had slouched down in the front seat and was trying to hide behind the dashboard – she blew me a kiss. Luckily, Mom was too busy keeping her eyes on the road, and Ruby was too busy keeping her eyes on herself in the rearview mirror to notice. Thank goodness! Ruby wouldn't have let me forget it.

I went to bed early that night to recover from my close encounters with love. How unlucky could I get? Three women in their eighties and then an eight-year-old girl falling in love with me, all in one afternoon. I suppose I should feel lucky that Ms. Hathaway wasn't among them. I drifted off to sleep, trying to understand just what Gran sees in horoscopes.

CHAPTER 6

The Karaoke Kid

Saturday, June 2
A little bit of glamour will do you a lot of good.
Throw yourself into the culture pool and fish
around for musical or artistic diversions.

I came down to breakfast looking anything but glamorous, with my hair sticking up in all directions as if I'd had a scare, which is exactly what I'd had. I had dreamed that I took my first girlfriend, who was eighty years old, hard of hearing, and named Ellie, to the school dance. But, worse than that, I found out toward the end of the dream that she was Ms. Hathaway's mother. I sat down at the breakfast table, hoping that my dream wasn't a premonition.

"Morning, Gran," I said.

"Bright colors suit you, Billy," she said, referring to my yellow sweatshirt.

Gran's about the only one who wouldn't think anything of it if I dyed my hair bright orange and went off to school looking like the shelf-stocker from the music store.

"Are you going hunting for Samuel Fogerty again today with Marjorie?" I asked, changing the subject.

"Yes, but we don't want to overdo it, dear. We have the Rock Climbing Club's annual ball tonight," she explained. "Marjorie and I want to dance the night away."

"Is there going to be a band?" I asked, in an attempt to keep Gran from talking about my horoscope for as long as possible.

"No, dear. Marjorie's granddaughter is taking care of the music."

I don't know why, but I imagined a pimply bespectacled girl wearing a lacy lime green dress.

"She's the DJ at Planet Rock," finished Gran.

Wow! I was impressed. It happened to be the weirdest, wildest nightclub around. You can't get in if you don't look like an oddball from outer space. It shouldn't have come as any surprise that

Marjorie's granddaughter worked there. Weird and wacky seem to run in the family.

"Enough of my day, Billy dear. It says in your stars that you're going to be the glamorous one today. Perhaps you could be our Prince Charming tonight at the Rock Climbing Club's ball," she said, chuckling.

Before I could answer, my wicked mother stepped into the kitchen and told me to hurry up and change, because she wanted Geena, Ruby, and me to go to the mall with her to look for a birthday present for Dad. But it wasn't easy getting ready in a hurry. My two mean sisters were hogging the bathroom, trying to make themselves look better in case they met their friends at the mall. I could have told them they were wasting their time.

An hour later, while we waited at a traffic light on the way to the mall, we saw Gran and Marjorie. They were busy stopping passersby and showing them a photograph of Samuel Fogerty. Gran had told me that she'd kept it in a box under her bed for over fifty years without Grandpa ever knowing about it. Samuel Fogerty had been her childhood sweetheart and an entertainer to the troops in the war. As we took off from the light, I saw a street performer pointing, with his violin bow, Gran and Marjorie in the direction of the City Mission for the Homeless.

"Keep an eye out for a parking spot, guys," said Mom, interrupting my thoughts. "It looks as if everyone has the same idea as us today."

While Ruby kept an eye out, Geena tried to hide in the front seat. She hated being seen out with the family. I carried on with my music immersion plan, which involved listening to my CD player. It would have been better to immerse myself in the music store at the mall, but I didn't care to show my face in there for a while.

"There's one, Mom," yelled Ruby.

After parking the car, we took the elevator up to the ground floor. I played my CD at just the right volume to drown out the elevator music but still hear Mom giving instructions. Unfortunately, I could also hear Ruby.

"Hey, look, there's going to be a karaoke demonstration at the mall," she cried, reading a poster in the elevator. "You could brush up on your singing, Billy."

"Ha, ha!" I snapped, knowing she meant my singing for the talent contest.

Then Ruby said something rotten. At least, I think she did by the look on her face. I'd turned up the volume so that I couldn't hear anything, not even Mom scolding Ruby, which might have been well worth listening to.

Little did I realize that the next thirty minutes would be more embarrassing than the last two days put together. As Ruby and I headed toward the menswear store to look for Dad's gift, Mom, who was taking Geena to buy jeans, yelled out to us, "No getting into trouble, you two. And, Billy, keep an eye on your sister!"

Looking back now, if only we'd made it to the menswear store without any detours, everything would have been fine. But Ruby and I went toward the arcade. Unfortunately, we never made it there either. Ruby wanted to watch the karaoke demonstration. She sat down in the front row and wouldn't budge. So, remembering how I was grounded for a week the last time I ignored Mom's "keep an eye on your sister" instructions, I really had to try to persuade her to leave. I started pulling and tugging at her. That's when the trouble started.

Ruby started pulling and tugging back at me, and the man on the stage, who was looking for volunteers to try out his karaoke machine, thought we were egging each other on to get up to sing. The next thing I knew, the man was pulling and tugging at *me*, directing me up the stairs, shoving a microphone into my hand, and telling me the words were up on the screen in front of me.

"Ladies and gentlemen, give a big hand to…"

He bent down to ask me my name.

I opened my mouth, but nothing came out.

"Billy. His name's Billy," shouted Ruby from the front row. She was loving watching me squirm.

"Give a big hand to Billy," continued the man.

What happened next wouldn't have if Gran and Marjorie hadn't stopped in the mall to buy the street performer a burger for helping them look for Sammy. At first I was thankful because it saved me from having to sing. Well, for a little while anyway. Gran, seeing me in trouble, grabbed the microphone out of my hand and dragged Marjorie and their friend up to sing on the stage, while nearly half the shoppers at the mall joined in. It was like a New Year's Eve party in June.

It ended up with Gran making Ruby and me sing along too. Gran handed me the microphone, thinking that the funny grin on my face meant that I was actually enjoying myself. I quickly threw it over to Marjorie, who took it with great gusto and started to sing off-key. She didn't have her reading glasses on and was making up the words as she went along. Unfortunately, the most embarrassing moment was yet to come.

Of all people to be shopping in the mall, there was Seth, looking like a hyena laughing his head off. But, worse still, next to the hyena was Ellie.

The trip home was quiet. Geena wasn't talking to any of us, particularly Gran, who had hitched a ride home with us while Marjorie stayed back at the karaoke stand to order a machine.

We all went our separate ways when we got home. Geena and Ruby went up to their rooms, Mom drove back to the mall to get Dad's present, and Gran and I watched the music channel on TV. She wanted to pick up the latest dance moves for the ball. Suddenly, Geena's yelling drowned out the music.

"Phone, Gran!" she hollered from upstairs.

All I heard was Gran's half of the conversation, but it didn't take me long to understand what it was all about.

"Hi, Marjorie dear… Oh, what a shame. I hope she feels better soon… And she is such a wonderful DJ… What a great idea. I'll see if he can do it… No problem. He's good at helping me out… OK then. We'll see you tonight at seven."

The next thing I knew, Gran had talked me into being the stand-in DJ for the ball and we were on our way to pick up Marjorie, whose granddaughter had come down with laryngitis. What I hadn't picked up at breakfast when I talked to Gran about the Rock Climbing Club's ball – even though she had said I could be Prince Charming – was that it was a costume ball. So now behind the wheel of *The Flying Beetle* was Cleopatra, alias Gran, and beside me in the back was Marjorie, dressed up as a wicked pirate. In the passenger seat was Marjorie's bowling partner, dressed as Napoleon Bonaparte. He owned the sound system they were going to use at the ball.

When we got there, they gave me my costume. When Gran had said I could be Prince Charming, I thought she was joking. She wasn't.

I got through the evening – just. Sammy would have said that it was good training for me. I suppose it *is* getting easier for me to make a fool of myself in front of hundreds of people.

Gran, Marjorie, Napoleon Bonaparte, and I were the last to leave. Since I was the DJ, I had to play music until the last guest left, which was well past when Cinderella dashed out. (Her babysitter had to go home at midnight.)

While the songs played, I had time to think about my music immersion plan and whether it was doing me any good: the music store, Geena's CDs, Ruby's dance class, karaoke, and now this – things were not going well at all. I suppose I'd just have to sing with Sammy tomorrow at the retirement home's concert after all. It was the closest thing I was going to get to a rehearsal.

The four of us finally left after Napoleon Bonaparte had packed up his sound system and we had helped him load it into the trunk. When my head finally hit the pillow around two o'clock, I went right to sleep.

CHAPTER 7

Napoleon Bonaparte on the Trail

Sunday, June 3
What you need more than anything else today is peace and quiet. And you'll definitely get it, so hang in there.

Apart from going down to breakfast a little later than usual, I began my morning just like any other. When I walked in the kitchen, Gran started reading me my horoscope. And, considering the way Gran was babbling on, it was already wrong.

"Billy love, you were a great DJ last night. You take after your grandfather. He could always do anything he tried. But, today, your reward is a little peace and quiet. No me. No Marjorie. What do you think of that?"

"Thanks, Gran," I mumbled into my bowl.

I was too busy worrying about Sammy's concert to eat. I pushed my cornflakes around with my spoon for ages before I told Gran that I was going over to Josh's. Then I shot out the back and biked over to the retirement home. Sammy was waiting for me when I got there.

"All right, kid. We're on last. So let's get in some practice," he said.

"Hear that clapping? That's what it's all about," he said as we made our way to the music room. By the time we were about to go on, my head was spinning. The waiting was killing me.

"Sammy, I can't go through with it," I said.

"You'll be fine. It's just nerves, kid. It happens to the best," he soothed.

"No, I *really* can't go through with it," I said.

"What's up, kid?"

"I can't do it, Sammy. It's Mom. She's over there," I said, pointing at the audience.

I had spotted Mom, who, luckily, hadn't seen me. She was sitting beside Mildred. I hadn't expected her to be there. It was her day off! But I suppose the concert was her idea after all.

"She'll start asking all kinds of questions. Then she'll find out about the talent contest," I said.

"Hey, we're on. They're calling us," Sammy cried. "Come on, kid."

"I can't! I just can't! Another time, Sammy," I replied, feeling really terrible about letting him down, but I just had to get out of there.

As I biked home, I spotted Ruby and Marisa playing at the park on their own. That is one of Mom and Dad's no-nos. It was just the sort of thing I could use to persuade Ruby to cough up what she knew about Seth.

"Marisa and I went into Seth's room to look for his basketball," Ruby said when she came home and I started questioning her.

"Yeah, so what?" I said.

"So, we saw something hanging up in his closet," she went on.

"What's so interesting about the contents of Seth's closet?" I snapped back.

"Who else do you know with a cat costume in their closet?" she replied. "Weird, huh?"

"Is that all?" I said. "Is that what you had to tell me? Big deal. I'm sure it's just part of his talent contest act – I already knew he was performing a cat song."

At that point, Ruby realized that what she had told me didn't even up the score. She begged me not to tell Mom and Dad about the park. In a moment of weakness, I agreed. But only after I got Ruby to agree to keep quiet about the contest.

So now that the danger of Mom and Dad finding out about the contest had passed, I settled down for a little peace and quiet. But I should have known horoscopes never come true.

Marjorie and Gran, now fully recovered from their night before, were full of energy, planning their next surveillance trip. Samuel Fogerty needed to be tracked down, even on a Sunday, they told me. They had gotten a lead when the street performer led them to the City Mission for the Homeless. But this time, they were being picked up by Napoleon Bonaparte. When he's not rock climbing and bowling, he's a private investigator. He owed Gran a favor for getting me to be the DJ.

"Hi, son. I hardly recognized you," he said when he arrived.

I was thinking the same thing.

"All right, Billy we're off. Tell your mother I'll be home for dinner. Toodle-oo!" called Gran.

In the afternoon, I still didn't get any peace and quiet. Ruby and her friends sang skipping songs outside at the top of their voices. Sisters are such a pain.

CHAPTER 8

Meow and Take a Bow!

Monday, June 4
You may feel dispirited and restless, but
don't allow your mood to spoil situations
that you find yourself in today. Brighter times
are immediately ahead.

Well, it had finally arrived. Talent contest day. I was still dwelling on yesterday's concert disaster when I sat down at the breakfast table.

"Cheer up, sweetheart," said Gran when she saw my expression. "Brighter times are ahead."

I glanced over and scanned the horoscopes with her. Why couldn't my sign be Scorpio? They were going to have a gift coming their way.

Gran was in a really good mood at breakfast. She and Marjorie were close to cracking the case, she said, thanks to their lead and Napoleon Bonaparte's contacts.

Sensing Mom was also in a good mood, I asked if I could go to Josh's place after school.

"I've been asked to stay over for dinner too," I fibbed.

"OK. Fine. Just call when you need me to pick you up," she replied. She seemed absorbed in her bagels, and she had a weird smile on her face. Goodness knows why bagels should be so funny. Mothers are strange sometimes.

So are teachers. Ms. Hathaway had a strange look on her face all morning – sort of like Dad when he spends too long with Gran. In fact, everyone seemed a little on edge – except for Seth.

When Christopher Preston, who was going to be the lighting manager for the show, popped into our classroom during the morning, I watched Seth closely the entire time. Seth never tried to get Christopher's attention. He didn't even seem interested in his visit at all, which was odd.

All through class, I felt dispirited, just as my horoscope had predicted. My music immersion plan had been a disaster. I had just embarrassed myself in front of Ellie every time. I was also restless. I needed to get to a phone so I could invite Sammy to the talent contest tonight. I couldn't very well turn up at Mom's work after school to ask him, since I was supposed to be at Josh's place.

When I finally got to a pay phone after school, a familiar voice answered, "Hello, Three Oaks Retirement Home, Grace speaking." I slammed down the receiver in a panic. I had to risk a visit.

When I got there, I sneaked around to Sammy's room and tapped on the window. No reply. I raced around to the dayroom. Sammy was snoozing in a chair near an open window.

"Psst! Psst!" I hissed. No answer.

"Hey, Sammy!" I said, a little louder.

This time, Sammy woke up.

"Hi there, kid. What are you doing here?" he asked, yawning.

"I came to see if you'd like to come to my concert," I whispered. "It starts at seven o'clock."

"Oh, if only it'd been another night. There's a jazz documentary at eight, and I'd hate to miss it."

If I'd just looked it up in the TV guide, I would have known there was no such program. I left the retirement home in a bad mood and raced back to the pay phone to call Gran and invite her and Marjorie to the concert.

Later that night, the mood was quite different backstage. Some people from another class were helping out Megan Butler with the props, and Christopher Preston had several helpers too.

Ms. Hathaway brought us all back to reality with a talk about winners, losers, and trying our best. I'm sure Megan Butler wasn't listening. Then, with a puff of smoke – well, it was dry ice actually – Ms. Hathaway vanished onto the stage.

The audience got a similar speech before she finally introduced the first contestant.

"She has made her costume, painted her own props, and has been singing in the shower, she tells me, since the age of four. Please welcome Megan Butler!" Trust Megan to be on first.

Christopher Preston then shone the spotlights on Megan. I took a quick look at the audience. That's when I caught sight of Gran and Marjorie in Row C, stumbling and apologizing as they tried to find seats in the dark. Maybe it wasn't such a good idea to have invited them. When Christopher dimmed the lights for special effects, all I could hear were hoots of laughter from Row C. I almost missed seeing the silhouette of Sammy sitting in Row H. What was he up to?

There was no time to think about it now. I whipped around and bumped into Seth.

"Sorry, Seth. I didn't see you," I apologized.

"Meeooww!" snarled the cat.

"Pardon?" I said, even though I had heard him.

"Meeooww, Billy!" he hissed.

That's when I figured it out.

Ms. Hathaway's dramatic introduction of Seth interrupted my thoughts. When one of Christopher's helpers shone the spotlights on Mungojerrie, he responded with a snarl. The cat wore a striped costume with face paint to match. Ms. Hathaway looked so proud.

Because I had been keeping an eye on Gran and Marjorie the whole time, I hadn't spotted Mom and Dad with Ruby. If I'd seen them there, I probably would have fainted. So, now that I think of it, it was probably for the best that I remained blissfully ignorant.

Eventually, my turn arrived. I was lucky last. Some luck! A swift shove from Megan Butler got me on stage one very long and quiet minute after Ms. Hathaway had introduced me. But I looked incredibly loud in my lime green tuxedo jacket. I had gone to the secondhand clothes store the day after Sammy's shopping spree, and I had managed to find the perfect outfit for a stand-up comedian. Gran and Marjorie were the only ones who laughed when I came on stage. You wouldn't have believed it. It was so unlike me.

"Ummm, good evening, ladies and gentlemen," I said in a voice that matched my outfit. "A funny thing happened to me on the way here tonight…"

It was a cliché, but true. In fact, some very peculiar things had happened over the past week, and I was beginning to see their funny side. Gran was rubbing off on me, and for once, I was glad. Things were looking up.

Gran and Marjorie were *far* from dispirited at the end of my performance. They were up on their seats yelling out, "Bravo! Bravo!" Even Ms. Hathaway had found some of my jokes funny.

But it was Ellie's laughing that pleased me the most. This time, she was laughing with me, not *at* me. Brighter times were here at last.

At the awards ceremony, there were some surprises in store. Megan placed third, and she didn't take it very well at all. The way Gran and Marjorie were calling out "Encore!" and whistling

at me, you would have thought I had come in first, not second. It was no surprise, though, that Mungojerrie won first place. The audience had lapped up his performance.

Mungojerrie came on stage for a short speech.

"Meeooww!" he hissed, then he disappeared as quick as a cat. I looked for Christopher Preston and Seth. Strangely, neither one of them was to be seen anywhere.

After the contest, Ms. Hathaway announced that supper would be served. I spotted Mom and Dad and was going over to explain about not telling them about the contest when I saw Marjorie's lips heading right for me. They were all puckered up and ready to go. Bull's-eye. She planted her Dewberry Dream lips right smack in the middle of my forehead.

Gran had spared me her usual – a hug that could suffocate a grizzly bear. She'd gone to talk to someone who was sitting not far behind her. Unfortunately, I wasn't spared Ruby. She was chomping down cookies near Mom, Dad, and Ms. Hathaway.

"You were awesome!" she cried, spraying a shower of crumbs over me. I could see Dad cringe.

"She's right," said Ms. Hathaway. "I have to say that Billy's far better at comedy than he is at poetry reading."

Mom kept listening to Ms. Hathaway sing my praises. It sounded like one of Mom and Mildred's conversations at the retirement home.

The next thing I knew, I felt a tap on my shoulder. It was Seth.

"You were great!" he said.

"Thanks," I said. "Christopher Preston was great too, wasn't he?"

It caught Seth off guard.

"How did you know?" he asked.

"Two things. Christopher Preston did the lighting for every act, except yours. And he called me Billy, not Billy-boy, like you always do."

"Are you going to tell?" Seth asked.

I was just about to answer him when Ellie interrupted us. She was still laughing at my last joke. Marjorie's granddaughter had told it to Gran, who had told it to me. Seth stood awkwardly for a while, not joining in, then he drifted off to search for Christopher Preston – no doubt to see if he'd blab.

"Do you want to go to a movie sometime?" Ellie asked when Seth had left.

"Ah… sure," I said. "That sounds great! But what about Seth? Aren't you two… well…"

"Yeah, but I was getting kind of bored. He's not funny like you," said Ellie. "I like a good laugh."

My mood was far from dispirited and restless when I finally collapsed into bed after the show. I had waited up for Gran, but, by midnight, I couldn't stay awake any longer. Then, at two o'clock, I sat up with a jolt. I'd just realized that, in my excitement over talking to Ellie, I hadn't seen Sammy after the show. I drifted back to sleep, promising myself I'd call him in the morning.

CHAPTER 9

Bingo!

Tuesday, June 5
The day may start with problems,
but it will end on a happy note.
Old and new friendships claim your attention.
A good period for affairs of the heart.

I got a sinking feeling when I went into the kitchen. Gran wasn't there. Even after a late night, she's always up at six. I looked outside and the newspaper was still where the carrier had left it. I raced upstairs to Gran's bedroom. The bed hadn't been slept in. I knocked on the bathroom door. No answer. I felt sick with worry.

"Mom! Dad!" I yelled, as I burst into their room. "Gran didn't come home last night."

"You know your grandmother, Billy," Mom said in a sleepy voice. She's probably at Marj's house. She'll call."

That gave me an idea. I raced down to the kitchen. All I got when I called Gran's cellular phone was a message saying she was out of the calling area. My mind was spinning. What if she'd been kidnapped by that person she went to talk to after the show? I frantically phoned Marjorie.

"Hi, Marjorie. It's Billy. Have you seen Gran?" I gasped. "She didn't come home last night."

"Sorry, dear, I haven't," she said. "I heard her say 'BINGO' last night, which was odd, because we usually play bingo on Wednesdays. Don't worry, Billy. You know your grandmother."

I knew it wasn't exactly out of character for Gran to go off without telling anybody, but I had a funny feeling that I couldn't shake. Mom let me stay home from school to wait for news.

At eight o'clock, the phone rang. But it was only Geena saying she'd be home after school. She'd stayed with a friend last night. She wouldn't be seen dead with her family at a school concert.

When we still hadn't heard from Gran by lunchtime, Mom started getting concerned. The police couldn't do anything. Gran hadn't been missing for twenty-four hours. But the police officer who had brought Gran back a week ago recognized our address. He said he'd try to help. Then I remembered Napoleon Bonaparte and called him. All I got was his answering machine. In a French accent, he said to leave a message.

Mom kept busy. She read the horoscopes. It's what Gran would have done. Tears tickled my eyes as I pictured Gran. I went over last night in my mind, trying to remember every little detail. When Mom read something in my horoscope about old and new friendships, my heart missed a beat, or it could have been because at that moment, I realized I hadn't called Sammy.

"Hello, Patti. It's Billy," I announced.

"Good afternoon, Billy. How can I help you?"

"Is Sammy there, please?"

"No, he isn't. Can I take a message?"

"Ummm, no thanks, Patti," I said.

When the phone rang as soon as I put it down, I jumped, then snatched up the receiver. "Gran! Is that you?" I bellowed. "Oh, hi, Ms. Hathaway, I'll get her." I handed the phone to Mom.

I could hardly hear what Mom said to her over the noise outside. A car was tooting its horn to the tune of the wedding march. I'd know that sound anywhere. It was *The Flying Beetle*.

"I've cracked the case, Billy," Gran yelled as she trotted up the driveway, her handbag swinging wildly. "I found Samuel Fogerty. We drove over to Westward Beach after the show last night. That's where we used to go swimming together. We talked and talked and talked and didn't realize the time. We ended up drinking coffee in an all-night café. I just came home to change and see if Marjorie wants to meet me and Samuel for a late lunch. Do you want to come?"

I was so glad to see Gran that I forgot to be mad at her, and I was so hungry that I said yes. Besides, I was bursting to meet Samuel Fogerty.

Even though I'd forgotten to be angry with Gran, Mom hadn't. She greeted Gran with one of Dad's "Ruby looks." Gran managed to sweet-talk her way into Mom's good graces again though.

An hour later, as we were walking into Bernie's Burger Bar with Marjorie, I started to feel faint.

I don't know if it was the stress of the past week, the lack of food, the fact that, only an hour ago I thought Gran was lying in a ditch, or just the sheer shock of seeing Gran's long-lost friend. You see, the man at the counter, Gran's Samuel Fogerty, war entertainer and childhood sweetheart, was none other than Sammy. Sammy Starbright. My very own Sammy. They were one and the same. I passed out.

It was the smell of Marjorie's cherry-flavored lip gloss only inches away from my face, the sound of smacking lips, and muffled talk about giving me mouth-to-mouth that brought me around fast.

"Hey, kid! Are you all right?" cried Sammy.

"Billy darling, you look awful," added Gran.

"You're as pale as one of my Pearl Luster lipsticks," consoled Marjorie.

Nothing in the last week came even close to being as shocking as that snippet of time in Bernie's Burger Bar. As Sammy and Marjorie helped me up to the counter, I wondered what could possibly happen next.

CHAPTER 10

The Winds of Change

Monday, September 24
A smooth day lies ahead, so make it
your business to relax and be less tense.
You can look to the future.
This is the start of new and exciting times.

"Here's the morning newspaper, Billy," said Mom when she came into the kitchen from outside.

"Thanks, Mom."

Things were back to normal. Well… almost. To make a long story short, I did stop being tense. That is, once I got used to things around here. Sammy ended up staying in our guest room for two months while he and Gran planned their wedding. Gran said she was too young to be hit by a bus or struck by lightning. In other words, she didn't want to live in the retirement home. So she made Sammy move in here. There are now two elderly people with creative streaks under our roof. Dad is more tense than ever.

Marjorie ended up being Gran's bridesmaid. She wore a pea green outfit. Her granddaughter, believe it or not, was one of Gran's flower girls. I've never seen a flower girl with hair that matched the bridesmaid's dress. It made Ruby look angelic.

Marjorie has just gone off to meet up with Gran and Sammy, who are taking a motorcycling honeymoon somewhere in Germany. They're all going to tour around France in a VW van. Marjorie's dying to see some *real* medieval castles.

Ellie and I are still friends. I don't know why, but she finds me funny. I'm glad I take after Gran's side of the family after all.

Ruby is still a pain. So is Megan Butler.

Mom and Dad are still Mom and Dad. Mom still looks after Mildred and all the other retirement-home residents, and Dad still scolds Ruby for talking with her mouth full of food. By the way, if you're wondering why Mom didn't know that Sammy's name was Fogerty, it was because the retirement home records show the surname Starbright. He legally changed his name after the war. He thought Fogerty sounded too old fogeyish.

My new teacher this year likes to give us poetry tests too, but he hasn't put together another talent contest. Not yet, anyway.

Christopher Preston is still trying desperately to make it into Seth's group. Oh, please!

And, as for Seth, well the Mungojerrie business seems like a long time ago. I don't know why I wanted to find out what he was up to. Who cares anyway!

Me? Well, I picked up where Gran left off. I read the horoscopes at breakfast every morning in her absence. But somehow, I don't think even the horoscopes will be able to predict what life will be like when Gran, Sammy, and Marjorie return. As Dad says, like the weather, there are some things you just can't predict!

From the Author

I really love seniors! My grandparents have been a huge part of my life, and my great-grandmother lived until the grand old age of ninety-six! Seniors love me too. I've got a loud booming voice that even Mildred could hear!

Like Billy, I wasn't crazy about talent contests and drama classes when I was a child. I hung up my ballet shoes at the tender age of six. There was no future for a heavy-hoofed, loud-voiced ballerina. At least now I can see the funny side of it.

My daughter Rosie has a zest for life that Gran, Marjorie, and Sammy would appreciate. She acts and dresses like Gran and has a voice as commanding as Ms. Munro's. That's why I wrote this book when everyone in my house was asleep!

Janine Scott